What happened next surprised even me.

Denny managed to be cool for about one solid minute, chewing thoughtfully. Then I guess he couldn't stand it any longer. "Uh . . . did any of you guys happen to notice that girl?" he asked.

"Which one?" Stephanie said innocently, glancing at Kate out of the corner of her eye.

"The one in the . . . uh . . . pink and green sweater," Denny said.

"Oh, that's Michelle Olsen," Stephanie replied. "She's a seventh-grader at Riverhurst Middle School, cheerleader, beauty queen . . . ," Stephanie began to rattle off Michelle's accomplishments.

But Kate interrupted her. "Michelle's going steady!" she said firmly.

"Oh." Denny picked up his slice of double-cheese pizza and bit into it again.

Somehow I didn't really believe that was the end of it. But what happened next surprised even me.

Look for these and other books
in the Sleepover Friends Series:

Kate's Surprise Visitor

Susan Saunders

AN
APPLE
PAPERBACK

SCHOLASTIC INC.
New York Toronto London Auckland Sydney

ISBN 0-590-42819-5

Copyright © 1990 by Daniel Weiss Associates, Inc. All rights reserved. Published by Scholastic Inc. APPLE PAPERBACKS is a registered trademark of Scholastic Inc. SLEEPOVER FRIENDS is a registered trademark of Daniel Weiss Associates, Inc.

12 11 10 9 8 7 6 5 4 3 2   0 1 2 3 4 5/9

Printed in the U.S.A.   28

First Scholastic printing, April 1990

Chapter 1

"A costume party at our age?!" Stephanie Green clunked her empty chocolate-shake glass firmly down on the table and shook her head. "Whoever dreams up the entertainment at Riverhurst Elementary has forgotten we're *not* little kids anymore."

"Come on, Stephanie, it'll be fun." Patti Jenkins took a last slurp of lime freeze before adding, "We'll think of something great the four of us can do together and come up with terrific costumes — you're good at that, Stephanie. . . ."

Stephanie sniffed. " 'Four Famous Characters from a Book?' " she asked. "Right, something really neat, like the Four Blind Mice. Or the Four Little Pigs. Or the Four Billy Goats Gruff. Or . . ."

1

"Nobody said it *had* to be fairy tales. What about the Four Musketeers?" I suggested — I'm Lauren Hunter.

It was a Friday afternoon, school was over for the week, and Stephanie, Patti, Kate Beekman, and I were sitting in our favorite booth at Charlie's Soda Fountain, finishing our usual drinks.

"No way," Stephanie said huffily. "We'd have to wear long wigs and knee boots. Then we'd look like total dorks! In fact, I may not go to the party at all."

"*You're* going to turn down a party — with *boys*?" Kate exclaimed as if she couldn't believe her ears.

"Fifth-grade boys? Who needs them!" Stephanie dismissed thirty or forty guys with a wave of her hand.

"So that's what you're so antsy about!" I said, the light suddenly dawning.

"What?" Patti asked, still puzzled, because Stephanie loves parties, and she's usually pretty enthusiastic about boys, too.

"The Riverhurst Middle School is having a dance the same night as ours . . . ," I began.

"So?" said Kate, peering quizzically at Stephanie.

2

Stephanie just shrugged her shoulders.

But I went on, "It's a Sadie Hawkins dance, isn't it?"

Stephanie sighed and gazed silently out the window.

"That means the middle school girls get to ask the boys," I said, "And Stephanie's pining away because of a certain blond seventh-grader."

"I'm not pining . . . ," Stephanie began crossly.

Kate groaned, "Steph-a-nie! After all the grief we've put up with from Donald Foster, how can you possibly be interested in *him*?!"

Donald Foster lives in the house between Kate's and mine, on Pine Street in Riverhurst. So naturally we've known him forever. He has spiky blond hair, green eyes, and kind of a cute smile. He's a seventh-grader, and to my mind, just about the most conceited person ever to walk the earth!

"Who else?" I said, grinning.

"Give me a break!" Kate said to Stephanie. "Donald Foster barely knows we're alive! What seventh-grader does?"

"Unless he's giving us a hard time about something," I added. Unfortunately Donald has been a witness to some of our most embarrassing moments.

3

"Yeah," Kate said, nodding. "Remember the morning we couldn't wash the purple gel out of our hair because the water was off, and Donald called us witches loud enough for everyone on Pine Street to hear? 'Looking good, girls! But where are your broomsticks?' " she bellowed like Donald had.

The waitress behind the counter jumped. Patti giggled nervously — she thinks Donald's sort of cute, too.

"Or the night he wanted to know if it was trendy for fifth-graders to look like the Slime Creatures in *Curse of the Radioactive Swamp?*" I reminded Stephanie. "Anybody with half a brain could see that we were only trying out some avocado beauty masks!"

"Or the time he told us we might as well give up on normal life and join the circus?" Kate said. "Just because we were keeping a poor, homeless donkey in the front yard." Kate paused for breath and went on. "Not to mention how vain Donald is! Remember when he gave himself a black eye? He was staring so hard at his reflection in a window on Main Street that he walked into the edge of a door!" Kate was really on a roll.

Stephanie bit her lip. "I don't care. He has lots of good qualities, too," she said. Then before I could

4

challenge her to name *one*, she blurted out, "It's just not fair! Michelle Olsen is asking Donald to the dance!" I don't know too many seventh-graders, but even I know who Michelle Olsen is. She's hard to miss. Michelle has honey-colored hair that waves naturally, big blue eyes, an incredible smile, and a fabulous wardrobe. She is definitely the biggest heartbreaker in the seventh grade.

"What do you mean, not fair?" Kate asked curiously.

"Well, it isn't," Stephanie replied. "Just because Michelle's a couple of years ahead of us, she gets to ask Donald Foster to a dance while I have to dress up like some kind of dweeb and let Mark Freedman and Larry Jackson tread all over my toes!"

"Mark happens to be an excellent dancer!" Kate corrected her. "And he's a lot nicer than any seventh-grader." Mark's a boy in our class who's kind of a friend.

"Yeah," I said. "And he isn't stuck-up like Donald either."

"Borrrrrrring! Anyway, everybody knows girls are at least two years ahead of boys at this stage," Stephanie said in this superior grown-up voice. "Which makes us far too old for fifth-graders. That

5

means Michelle's too old for Donald, while I'm just the right age. After all, eleven plus two does equal thirteen."

Kate, Patti, and I exchanged glances. The addition was right, but there was plenty wrong with Stephanie's reasoning.

"Stephanie, thirteen minus two is *zero*, as far as seventh-graders are concerned," Kate said. I agreed that was a lot closer to the truth.

Stephanie paid no attention. "What's so great about Michelle Olsen, anyway?"

"Except a permanent tan, double-pierced ears, and terrific hair," I mumbled, pushing my own straggly brown bangs out of my face.

"And a figure," Kate pointed out.

But Stephanie ignored us both and pressed on: "I mean, I don't think I'd mind if Cathy Ryan or Amy Hoff asked Donald to the dance, because they're so nice and . . ."

"They look more like fifth-graders," Kate murmured to me. Cathy and Amy are both kind of short for seventh grade, and they have about as much of a shape as I do, which is to say, the same as your average string bean.

"But Michelle will . . . will *destroy* poor Donald," Stephanie wailed. "She'll break his heart! I just know it!"

"Hold on — isn't Michelle going steady with Jimmy Coleman?" I asked.

Stephanie sighed. "She was for about ten minutes. And she was going with Gary Sobel before that" — Gary's captain of the middle school soccer team — "and before that there was Steve Quinn" — pitcher on the baseball team — "and Chuck Morris" — the best junior high basketball player in the county. "By the end of the year, she'll have gone steady with all the coolest boys in the seventh grade!" Stephanie sounded truly upset. "Poor Donald. . . ."

"Listen, Stephanie," Kate tried again. "Sixth grade is a kind of dividing line. We're on one side, and Donald is miles away on the other. It won't do you any good to get all worked up about him and Michelle because — "

"I don't agree," Stephanie interrupted. "I think of Donald as a friend. Wouldn't you try to save a friend from making a bad mistake?"

"I *am* trying to save a friend!" Kate said. "*You!* Anyway, if Donald can be interested in a girl who acts as dippy as Michelle . . ." Her voice trailed off.

"That's right," I said. "She starts posing like a

beauty queen if there's a cute boy within ten miles!"

"And what about that business she does with her face?" Kate added. Michelle has this way of pouting her bottom lip out and opening her eyes really wide whenever there's a guy around. "If Donald's taken in by that hokey routine, then the two of them deserve each other!"

"I knew I should never have told you!" Stephanie said crossly. "Donald Foster happens to be a terrific — "

"Are you sure Michelle is asking Donald and not Jimmy?" Patti broke in quickly, before Kate or I could start arguing with Stephanie about Donald's terrific-ness.

Stephanie nodded gloomily. "I heard her say so just last night. I drove over to Romanos with Dad, to pick up some baby formula for the twins" — Stephanie has a new little baby brother and sister — "and Michelle was in the makeup section, with Stacy Bennett. I wanted to check out the lip gloss anyway, so — "

"Your mom won't let you wear lip gloss!" Kate said sternly.

"I know, I know! Or get my ears pierced, either, but that doesn't mean I can't at least *think* about it!"

Stephanie replied. "Anyway, Michelle and Stacy were talking about the Sadie Hawkins dance next Friday. Stacy said that she was going to ask Neal Curry — you know, that new pitcher on the baseball team. Then Michelle started smirking and she said, 'I think I'll make Donald Foster's day.'" Stephanie had widened her eyes and copied Michelle's drawl. "'Donald's been hanging around me like . . . like a *puppy* for weeks! And he *is* kind of cute.' *Kind* of cute! Can you believe it? Then Stacy said, 'But what about Jimmy?' and Michelle said, 'Jimmy who?' and snickered!"

"Oh, brother!" I muttered. I was tempted to feel a little sorry for Donald myself. He wasn't going to know what hit him!

"Michelle also said she wanted to ask Donald to the dance face-to-face — that way she could see exactly how *thrilled* he was." Stephanie looked dismal. "That means she probably cornered him at school this morning," she finished.

Kate shook her head. "Nope, not this morning she didn't. Donald's at home with a strep throat. Mrs. Foster called my mom during breakfast to ask if she'd mind running over to see if he needed anything while Mrs. Foster went out shopping."

9

"So Michelle will just trap him on Monday," Stephanie pointed out glumly.

"I think they're perfect for each other. Michelle's even more conceited than Donald is, if that's possible," Kate said. "But then, I think most seventh-graders are too full of themselves to be real, anyway, especially seventh-grade *boys!*" She shook her head. "And *I'm* going to have one living in my house for ten whole days!"

Now we were on to Kate's problem. I sighed. Wasn't *anyone* interested in the costume party?!

"Maybe he won't be as bad as all that," Patti said encouragingly.

"He's already ruined my weekend," Kate said. "I was planning to spend Saturday and Sunday afternoons at the foreign film festival at the Quad!" Kate's a real movie freak. Foreign, all-American, black and white, color, silent, musical — if it's on a screen, she'll watch it. She'd like to be a movie director some day, and she takes her movies very seriously. "Only now I have to entertain Denny, instead." She sounded disgusted. "Denny Bright — if you say it fast enough, he sounds like a *toothpaste*."

"Why isn't Denny in school?" Stephanie asked.

"I guess holidays in Canada are different from

ours," Kate said with a disinterested shrug. "Dr. Bright is coming to Central County Hospital for a job interview. He and Dad have been best friends since medical school and Dad talked him into checking out the job. Of course, Dad also insisted he stay with us while he was here. Then Dr. Bright called yesterday to say he'd decided to bring his family along, to see how they'd like Riverhurst. So Dad had to invite them *all* to our house."

"If your dad and Denny's are such good friends, why haven't you met the Brights before?" I wanted to know. It seemed pretty strange to me — I see my best friends practically every day!

"Because as soon as he graduated from med school, Dr. Bright moved with his wife to this little town so far out in the wilds of Canada that you practically have to travel by dog sled to get there," Kate said. "According to Dad, Dr. Bright was always crazy about the great outdoors."

"And now the Brights are thinking of moving *here*?" Patti asked in a surprised voice. She had a point. Riverhurst isn't as crowded as the city, but it's not exactly the great outdoors, either — unless your idea of getting back to nature is sitting on a park bench under an elm tree.

11

"Yes, because the school in Moose Jaw — that's the town in Canada — stops after the seventh grade," Kate explained. "Denny would have to go away to boarding school next year. His parents really don't want to split the family up, and since Dad was always writing to Dr. Bright about them working to-gether . . ." Kate took a sip of her float.

"So Denny might be living here permanently?" Stephanie asked. "And he's a seventh-grader."

"Don't remind me," Kate said.

"Maybe he'll get to be best friends with Donald Foster," Stephanie said thoughtfully. "And if we're good friends with Denny, naturally we'll get to be better friends with . . ."

"Dream on," muttered Kate.

But before Stephanie could really get rolling about Denny and Donald and the four of us — she's a world-class planner — Patti whispered excitedly, "Look! It's Michelle Olsen!"

A bunch of middle school kids were clustered on the sidewalk just outside our window. Chuck Morris was there wearing his basketball sweater and towering over everybody else. He was grinning so hard his jaws must have ached. Jimmy Coleman was next to him, talking a mile a minute while he smoothed the back of his hair down over and over again. Steve Quinn was shifting from one foot to the other, just waiting to get a word in edgewise. Two or three other boys I didn't recognize were skulking around the edge of the group, trying to get closer to the middle. And smack in the center was the focus of all this attention: Michelle Olsen, natch.

Her thick wavy hair hung to her shoulders. Lime-green ribbons were woven into two little braids on either side of her face. From our window seat we were close enough to see the gold earrings that gleamed in her pierced ears — little hearts in the top holes and flowers in the bottom ones.

"Hearts and flowers *and* Perilous Peach lip gloss," Stephanie said gloomily. "I saw her buying it last night at Romanos."

"Maybe Michelle's asked Jimmy to the dance after all. Or Chuck," Patti told Stephanie soothingly. "Chuck's looking pretty happy."

As a matter of fact, all the boys had goofy grins on their faces, as Michelle favored first one and then another with her dazzling smile.

Stephanie shook her head. "She said it would be Donald, and she meant it," she muttered hopelessly. "If I could only think of a way to save him . . ."

13

"Here she comes," Kate warned.

". . . Miss America . . . ," I sang under my breath, the way they do in the beauty pageant on TV.

Michelle Olsen strolled up the sidewalk as if she'd already been crowned queen. She waltzed around the corner, strolled through the front door of Charlie's, and disappeared into the first booth. There was practically a riot as four or five boys fell all over themselves trying to sit next to her.

"Let's go before I get totally depressed," Stephanie said in a low voice. "I'm afraid Michelle's going to break Donald's heart, no matter what I do!"

Chapter
2

When it came to the Donald Foster situation I basically agreed with Kate. The main thing Donald needed saving from was his own conceited self! It seemed to me that maybe a small setback in his life now and then would do him some good.

Besides, I didn't want to think too much about Donald Foster or Denny Bright. We only had a week to come up with fabulous costumes for the party! And they absolutely had to be fabulous. I couldn't stand to listen to Jenny Carlin bragging through the rest of fifth grade about how she'd won first prize, whatever it was.

Jenny's kind of a Michelle-in-training. She and I have been sworn enemies ever since the beginning of the year, when Pete Stone decided he was interested in me instead of Jenny.

Not that I did anything to make him interested, and it only lasted for a couple of weeks. But Jenny's never forgiven me for it. She never misses a chance to get in a dig at me, either: like at lunch that day in the school cafeteria.

I was minding my own business, when all of a sudden I heard this voice. "My costume is an original — and it's being handmade!" Jenny practically screeched to her best, and only, friend, Angela Kemp, in the lunch line. "It's a secret, but . . . I'm going as half of a famous couple." Jenny cocked an eye in my direction. "And I've talked Pe-e-ete" — she managed to make his name sound like it was about ten syllables long — "into going as the other half!"

"Jack and Jill, after they fall down the hill," Kate murmured to me. We both giggled. But I started thinking. Handmade, original costume or not, wasn't it up to the Sleepover Friends to give Jenny and Pete some *friendly* competition?

After all, Kate, Stephanie, Patti, and I would obviously do something together. All four of us are in 5B, Mrs. Mead's class at Riverhurst Elementary.

16

And we spend almost all of our spare time after school and on weekends together. We also take turns having sleepovers every Friday night. With us, it's one for all and all for one. Why should the costume party be any different?

In the beginning, though, it was just Kate and me. Since we're practically next-door neighbors on Pine Street, Kate and I started playing together while we were still wearing diapers. By the time we were in kindergarten we were best friends. That's when the sleepovers started. Every Friday, either Kate would spend the night at my house, or I'd stay over at the Beekmans'. It got to be such a regular thing that Dr. Beekman, Kate's dad, named us the Sleepover Twins.

Not that we're really very much alike. Kate's short and blonde. I'm tall with brown hair. Kate's incredibly neat; I'm definitely messy. Kate's sensible, while I've been known to let my imagination run away with me. But in spite of our differences — or maybe even *because* of them — Kate and I spent thousands of hours together without a single major disagreement.

In the old days, we'd dress up in our moms' clothes and play Grown-Ups and School at our sleepovers. Or we'd "cook," which meant melting s'mores all over the toaster oven, or filling up the ice-cube trays with cherry Kool-Aid.

Luckily, our cooking improved as we got older. Kate came up with a dynamite recipe for marshmallow super-fudge, and I invented a delicious dip that goes with everything from blue-corn chips to Chee-tos. When we weren't cooking or eating, we watched movies on TV nonstop, or made up our own Mad Libs, or played endless games of Truth or Dare. Sometimes we'd spy on my older brother, Roger, and his friends, or think up ways to keep Kate's little sister, Melissa, from spying on *us*.

We had other friends at school, of course, and around the neighborhood. But the Friday night sleepovers were always just the two of us.

Then, the summer before last, Stephanie Green moved from the city into a house at the other end of Pine Street. Stephanie and I got to know each other because we were both in Mr. Civello's fourth-grade class last year.

Stephanie was great. She told neat stories about her life back in the city, and she knew all the latest dances and fashions. She'd already worked out her own style of dressing, too, which is pretty amazing for a fourth-grader. She almost *always* wears red, black, and white — colors that look fantastic with her curly black hair. I thought Stephanie was special, and I wanted Kate to get to know her, too. So I invited Stephanie to a sleepover at my house.

Talk about a major disaster! Kate thought Stephanie was a total airhead who only cared about clothes. And Stephanie was convinced that Kate was a stuffy know-it-all. My brother, Roger, said the problem was obvious: "They're too much alike — both bossy!"

Whatever the reason, the two of them didn't exactly hit it off. But I wasn't about to give up. Kate was my best friend, and I liked Stephanie a lot, too. I was going to make them like each other, even if it took forever!

Since all three of us live on Pine Street, it was only natural that we'd ride our bikes to school at more or less the same time every day. I made sure it was at *precisely* the same time. I also arranged it so that Kate and I ran into Stephanie at the mall a couple of Saturdays in a row. Then when Stephanie asked me to spend a Friday night at her house, I said

I absolutely had to bring Kate along, because we *always* spend Friday nights together. I just gave Kate another version of the same story.

At the Greens', Stephanie's mom had made a big platter of her yummy peanut-butter-chocolate-chip cookies. That softened Kate up a little. Then we watched three movies in a row on Stephanie's private TV, which didn't hurt, either. The very next week, Kate invited Stephanie to a sleepover at her house.

"It's only polite," Kate said. "She asked me over first." But I knew I had won!

Not that Kate and Stephanie suddenly saw eye-to-eye about everything, not by a long shot. Half the time, I'd end up caught in the middle. Which is just one of the reasons I was glad when Patti turned up in Mrs. Mead's class this year.

Patti's from the city, too, but she's not a bit like Stephanie. She's much quieter, even a little shy sometimes. Patti's also kind, thoughtful, and one of the smartest kids at school. Best of all, she's great at heading off arguments.

Kate and I both liked her right away, so when Stephanie wanted Patti to be part of our gang, we were all in total agreement. School had barely started this year, and suddenly there were *four* Sleepover

Friends — and we really do look out for each other.

That Friday we finished up our drinks, and the four of us quickly ducked around Charlie's candy counter so Stephanie wouldn't get totally burned out about Michelle. Then we zoomed out the door to the bicycle rack.

"About our costumes . . . ," I began as I unlocked my bike.

"We'll just put on some sheets and go as ghosts! There are plenty of ghosts in books," Kate said grumpily.

Put on some sheets?! Had Kate gone crazy? Jenny Carlin in a handmade original, and me in one of my mom's faded old top sheets?

"Why don't we stop off at that rental place?" Patti suggested. "You know — Creative Costumery. It's only a few blocks out of our way. Maybe instead of putting together our costumes ourselves, we can *rent* something really outstanding!"

"That's a great idea!" I said. At least somebody was taking the situation seriously. "Jenny Carlin, here we come!"

But Stephanie shook her head. "Not now," she said heavily. "I have too much on my mind."

"Ditto," Kate said. "Anyway, I have to go clear

out my bedroom so that Dr. and Mrs. Bright can move into it. They're driving out from the city early this evening." She ticked off on her fingers: "Denny gets the spare bedroom, his little sister gets Melissa's other bed. And *I* get the living room couch."

"As much as I'd like to, I can't go now, either," I suddenly remembered. "I have the basement to deal with."

"Still?" Stephanie asked as we pedaled up Main Street toward Hillcrest. "How long does it take to clean out a basement?"

"Well, you figure stuff has been collecting down there for at least seventeen years . . . ," I said glumly. "It's going to take a couple more days just to go through it all." I really wasn't looking forward to finishing the job. My mom's started working again, full-time. I help out by doing chores around the house, but the basement was turning out to be a major, major chore! "And if I have time I'll also stir up some snacks for tonight," I added. It was my turn to have the sleepover that Friday.

"Then maybe I'll stop by Creative Costumery myself," Patti said. She slowed down as we reached the corner of Main Street and Hillcrest. "At least I can find out what it would cost."

"Excellent!" I said. "But let's stay away from gorilla suits . . . okay? I really don't want to be a gorilla, although there are at least four gorillas in *Gorillas in My Luggage* by that zoo writer. Also, I don't think I'm willing to be a vegetable . . . what about you guys?"

But Kate and Stephanie didn't hear me. They had already disappeared around the corner in a heavy fog of gloom.

"Don't worry, Lauren," Patti said comfortingly. "The sign at Creative Costumery says *No party too big or too small*. I bet they'll have the perfect outfits for us. I'll tell you all about it tonight."

Thank goodness for Patti! If it were up to Kate and Stephanie, we probably wouldn't even *have* costumes!

Chapter
3

My mom is a saver. She still has some dresses from when she was in junior high. She'd also rate at least a seven on the Messy Scale of one to ten. Add in my dad, with all of his gadgets that no longer work, but that he *might* have the time to fix some day. And Roger's treasures, like every one of his old, torn Little League uniforms. Not to mention practically every toy and picture book *I've* ever owned. Mix it all together and you've got a humongous crisis in the basement. I'd been working down there all that week, and I'd barely scratched the surface.

We'd rented a dumpster from the garbage company, and I would throw three or four boxes full of junk into it every afternoon. Then Mom and Dad and Roger would dig through it when they got home, and half the stuff would end up back where it started. I was beginning to think I'd be cleaning out the basement for the rest of my life!

On their way into my house that night, Kate and Patti checked the dumpster out, too.

"Are you kidding?! This is a great camera!" Kate said, holding up somebody's ancient Kodak that had probably been broken for at least twenty-five years.

"Would you mind if I kept this?" Patti had found a ratty old teddy bear of Roger's with one ear missing. "He looked so sad, sitting in the garbage."

The three of us were in my kitchen, sipping Dr Peppers, eating chips, and waiting for Stephanie to show up, so the sleepover could officially begin.

"As long as you take your great finds *home* with you, be my guest," I said, wiping off a blob of my special dip — onion soup, olives, sour cream, and bacon bits — that I'd spilled on my sweatshirt. "Now, Patti, tell me what you found out at Creative Costumery!"

"No good," Patti replied sadly. "To rent one costume for one day costs twenty dollars! And that doesn't even include the cleaning bill."

25

"Forget it," I said, seriously disappointed. "My allowance would be wiped out for months!" The image of Jenny Carlin in a gorgeous evening gown and me in a bed sheet made me so weak that I slumped onto a chair. I was beginning to feel as gloomy as Stephanie and Kate.

"Did the Brights come yet?" Patti was asking her.

"No, but Dad expected them to arrive any minute. I can hardly wait," Kate said woefully.

"You could always move in with us if it got too close for comfort," I offered.

"I'd do it in a flash, but my parents have already warned me about not being 'gracious,' " Kate said. "And moving out probably wouldn't be gracious, do you think?"

Stephanie strolled into the kitchen, carrying her red canvas tote full of overnight stuff in one hand and a blue thermos in the other.

"Hot chocolate?" I asked, pointing at the thermos. Mrs. Green makes great hot chocolate with a dash of cinnamon in it. "Or a peanut-butter-smoothie?" That's a sleepover special, and one of my all-time favorite drinks.

But Stephanie shook her head. "Nope," she said. "Chicken soup."

"Chicken soup?" Kate, Patti, and I exclaimed at the same time.

"Since when is *chicken soup* a sleepover snack?" asked Kate, staring at Stephanie.

"It's supposed to be good for . . . sore throats and fevers, isn't it?" Stephanie mumbled, refusing to meet Kate's eye. "Have you got some kind of container to pour this into, Lauren? A thermos just doesn't look very special."

I was still knocked for a loop by the chicken soup! "You cooked for Donald Foster?" I croaked.

"As a matter of fact, my mom cooked the soup for our dinner tonight," Stephanie said breezily. "I just added a couple of touches of my own, to make it tastier."

Patti took a big green bowl with a cover down from one of the cabinets, and Stephanie poured as much of the soup into it as she could fit. Then she snapped the cover on tight.

"You're not seriously planning to waltz over to Donald's to present it to him?" Kate said, both eyebrows raised.

"Certainly not," Stephanie replied. "I'm leaving it on the Fosters' back porch, along with a get-well card. . . ." She paused. "Although the sooner he gets well, I guess the sooner Michelle will get *him*." She shrugged hopelessly. "Anyway, when Mrs. Foster opens the door to let Fluffy in she'll see it and . . ." Fluffy is the Fosters' big red cat.

"How did you sign the get-well card?" I asked her.

" 'From your friends next door,' " Stephanie said.

"Gross!" Kate yelped. "Donald will think the soup's from Lauren and me!"

"Never fear. The next time I see him, I'll be sure to ask him how he liked *my* soup," Stephanie said, sounding a little touchy. She pulled a brightly colored card out of her tote and laid the bowl on top of the covered bowl. Then she picked it up and headed for my back door. "Please get the door for me, Lauren. I'll be right back."

"I can't believe she's doing this!" Kate said as we watched Stephanie walk slowly across my backyard toward the hedge, carrying the big green bowl of soup. "All this for *Donald Foster*?!"

"I don't think it's Donald, as much as it's Stephanie wishing she were older," Patti said softly. "Compared to the twins, Stephanie must feel almost like a grown-up! I think she's just trying to prove that she's not a little kid anymore."

Maybe Patti was right. Stephanie *had* been talking an awful lot lately about lip gloss, and pierced ears, and heels. And that business about eleven plus two equals thirteen? Donald is practically the only seventh-grade boy who ever speaks to us — even if it's only to tease — and he's handy, living on Pine Street. So it's only natural he'd be the person Stephanie focused on.

"Lauren, did I hear the door open?" my mom called from the living room, where she and my dad were watching TV.

"Uh — yes," I answered. "Stephanie stepped outside for a second."

"All right, but no wandering around in the dark, honey — you know the rules," Mom said.

"We won't," I told her. I meant it at the time.

"Stephanie's coming back," Patti reported from the door. "Without the soup."

Stephanie clattered up the back steps and into the kitchen again. "Mission accomplished," she said in a low voice. "I left the bowl on the Fosters' doormat. And I heard Donald coughing away, so chicken soup should be perfect!"

"Now that Donald is taken care of, can we please go upstairs and get on with our sleepover?" Kate said.

I started piling some sleepover necessaries on our largest tray: a king-size bottle of Dr Pepper, the dip I'd just made, and a huge bag of chili-flavored potato chips. "Yes and we can start working out our costumes," I said. "We'll definitely have to design our own, somehow. We sure can't afford to pay eighty dollars for the four of us!"

"Eighty dollars!" Stephanie exclaimed. She tore open the chip bag and snared a few. "Maybe *all* of us ought to stay at home!"

I glared at her. "And let Jenny — and Pete Stone — walk away with first prize, whatever it is?" I said firmly. "No way!"

Kate added a pile of napkins and some glasses to the tray, and the four of us headed upstairs to my bedroom.

"Want to watch *Friday Chillers*?" Kate said, reaching for the portable TV as soon as I'd set the tray down. Clearly, her mind wasn't on the costume party, either.

"Hang on. I have something to show you guys first," Stephanie said. She reached into her red canvas tote and pulled out a large gray envelope with "Teen Make-Overs" printed on it in big, shocking-pink letters.

"Stephanie, I don't know if I'm in the mood to smear makeup all over my face, and then spend an hour washing it off," Kate told her.

"This isn't make*up* . . . it's make-*overs*!" Stephanie opened the envelope and pulled out a bunch of thick sheets of paper.

"We're going to play paper dolls?" I asked, because from where I was standing, all I could see was a whole page of different kinds of hairstyles, waiting to be punched out. Paper dolls didn't quite seem to fit in with Stephanie's new grown-up attitude.

"Lau-ren!" Stephanie said with an impatient shake of her head. "Just watch, okay?" She leafed through the sheets, until she came to a page covered with the outlines of faces. There were just little dots in the centers for noses, and they had necks, of course. But otherwise, the faces were blank.

"You choose the face shape most like your own," Stephanie explained. "Round, oval, squarish, or heart-shaped. You pick out your eyes from here."

She held up a sheet of perfectly round eyes, oval eyes, and almond-shaped eyes in blue, green, and brown. "Then you try out different hairstyles, eyebrows, and lips from these sheets." She spread the sheets out on the floor for us to look at. The page of lips was truly amazing — every size, shape, and color!

"Wow!" said Patti, checking out the eyebrows. "Where did you get this stuff?"

"I ordered it from the back of *Teen Topics*," Stephanie replied. *TT* — which is what we call it for short — is just about our favorite magazine this year. Even Kate was impressed.

"It *is* kind of neat," she admitted, studying the hairstyle page. "I've always wondered how I'd look with French braids." Kate's hair is short, kind of brushed back at the front and on the sides.

"Your face is oval," Stephanie said, gazing at Kate. She punched out one of the outlines. "Here — " she pulled a felt tip pen from her tote — "I'll just sketch in your nose. . . ." Stephanie's a really good artist. She put in a few lines for cheeks, too, and in a few seconds the oval punch-out looked quite a bit like Kate, at least around the middle of the face.

Stephanie sketched a nose and cheeks on another oval for me. Then she did a squarish cut-out face for Patti, and a round one for herself.

Kate was busy sliding a punch-out of long hair in French braids onto her outline. She picked out a pair of almond-shaped green eyes to match her own. Then she added some thin, arched eyebrows and full, dark-red lips.

"Wow!" I said. "You look just like Selena Latham!" Selena Latham plays a truly evil character on *Houston*, on Channel Six at eight o'clock on Mondays.

"I guess it *is* a little much," Kate said with a grin. She changed the spiky eyebrows to slightly curved ones, and chose a smaller set of lips, in light pink. "Here, Lauren," she said. "You try the red ones." She pushed them toward my oval face.

She seemed to have forgotten all about Denny Bright. Stephanie's make-overs were a great idea!

While we snacked on chips and dip, we took turns giving ourselves long blonde hair, curly red hair, and short black hair. We traded curvy red lips, pouty pink lips, and pale-peach puckered lips. I tried out arched eyebrows, straight eyebrows, eyebrows that slanted up, and ones that slanted down.

Then we started to run low on soda and munchies. Running low on food and drink at a sleepover always makes me uneasy — I *like* to eat. In fact, Kate and Stephanie sometimes call me the Endless Stomach because I have such a healthy appetite.

"I'm going down to the kitchen to get more chips," I announced. "And I think there's some cherry vanilla ice cream in the freezer, if anyone's interested."

"I'll help you," said Patti.

We left Stephanie and Kate hunched over their work, exchanging eyebrows, lips, and hair, and crept down the dark stairs — my parents were already in bed for the night.

"Grab some of that chocolate syrup," I told Patti as I opened the freezer for the ice cream. I'd just set it down on the counter when I noticed Stephanie's thermos.

I picked it up and jiggled it. The thermos felt about a third full. "I wonder how Mrs. Green's chicken soup is?" I murmured.

"If it's half as good as her peanut-butter-chocolate-chip cookies . . . ," Patti said.

"I think I'll give it a taste," I said opening the silverware drawer for a spoon. "I love homemade chicken soup."

I unscrewed the thermos and poured some of the soup into the top. "It's still warm. And it smells terrific." I scooped up a spoonful and popped it into my mouth.

"Mmm . . . ," I said, sort of swishing the warm soup over my tongue.

Then I swallowed. . . . "AAAAAGH!" I managed to squawk, just before I started coughing my head off! "Hot!" I croaked around coughs. "Hot! Hotttt!"

Patti turned on the cold water in the sink, full-blast. I grabbed the sprayer, stuck it in my mouth, and squirted.

I drank long and hard. When my throat finally stopped feeling as though I'd swallowed a red-hot coal, I turned the water off.

"Stephanie's been fooling around with tabasco sauce!" I rasped to an anxious-looking Patti.

Chapter
4

"Oh, no!" Patti said. "Not again!" Stephanie once made some chili that was so spicy it practically roasted our taste buds. "If Donald Foster drinks that soup, he'll never forgive her!"

"You mean he'll never forgive *Kate and me*!" I said. I turned the water back on because my throat was still smoldering. "Remember what the card said: 'From your friends *next door*.' Get Stephanie and Kate, okay?"

Patti dashed silently up the stairs while I squirted about a gallon of cold water into my mouth. She came back down with Kate and Stephanie in a flash.

"What's the matter?" Stephanie said when she saw me with the spray.

"Just how much tabasco did you add to the soup to make it *tastier*?" I asked accusingly.

Stephanie shrugged. "Not more than a drop or two — chicken soup can be awfully blah."

"More like a drop or fifteen!" I growled. "I don't think tabasco is such a great idea for somebody with a sore throat."

Kate shook her head. "People with strep throat can only eat soothing things, like ice cream, or Jell-O, or absolutely bland soup." Kate knows a lot of medical stuff, because of her dad. "Tabasco would make Donald . . ."

"Cough his head off?!" I asked, my throat still in flames.

Kate suddenly caught on. "At the very least! Then he'll read the dumb get-well card, and think you and I did it on *purpose*, Lauren! We better do something *now*!" She raced for the back door. I was right behind her.

"What about what your mom said?" Patti whispered. She was hard on my heels as we hurried down the back steps.

"If my mom catches us outside, she'll ground me for a few weeks," I replied in a low voice. "If Donald bathes his tonsils in that tabasco soup . . .

he'll be on our cases for the rest of our *lives*!''

''Sorry, guys.'' Stephanie caught up with Kate, Patti, and me at the hedge. She looked crushed. ''I guess I overdid the sauce a little, huh?''

''Oh, well,'' Kate murmured. ''It's not the end of the world. Maybe we'll get lucky with Donald, for once.''

When we'd squeezed through the bushes between my house and Donald's, though, my mom's green bowl was no longer sitting on the doormat at the top of the Fosters' back steps! We couldn't see Donald's window, because it is on Kate's side of the house, but the kitchen and living room lights were burning brightly.

''We're doomed,'' I whispered to Kate.

''Not necessarily,'' Stephanie said. She crept out of the hedge, keeping to the darkest shadows, and darted to the far side of the Fosters' house. She was back in a flash to report: ''I think we're okay.'' ''Donald's lamp is off, which probably means he went to bed early. *Before* I dropped off the soup!''

Patti nodded. ''I don't hear any coughing.''

''Right!'' Stephanie said. ''And nobody would want to eat chicken soup for breakfast. I'll just get my mom to call Mrs. Foster before lunch and tell her there was a mistake in the recipe! That way there won't be any problem!"

Then Kate hissed, "Listen — they're here!"

My skin began to crawl, because that's an exact line from *Fiends from the Fire Galaxy*, an old sci-fi movie we'd watched a few weeks before at Stephanie's. Sometimes I do have a runaway imagination, especially at night. "*Who's* here?!" I managed to whisper.

"The Brights!" she said. "Come on!"

Patti, Stephanie, and I followed Kate as she tiptoed toward her own hedge. Now I could hear people talking in the Beekmans' driveway, too.

"How long has it been, Dermit?" It was Kate's dad's voice. "Ten years? Twelve?"

"At least! It's great to see you!" A man's voice boomed. "This is Denny . . . and this is Sara. Dr. and Mrs. Beekman, kids."

We wriggled into the hedge and peered through the branches, trying to make out the visitors without much success. They were between us and the Beekmans' porch light, and dark shapes were about all we could manage.

Kate's mom and dad and the Brights began unloading a big pile of suitcases from the Brights' car.

"It looks like they plan to stay with us for a year or two!" Kate grumbled as we tried to get comfortable in the lilacs.

Suddenly, there was a loud *"meow!"* from somewhere in Kate's yard.

"It's Fluffy!" Kate said.

"Shoo! Go away!" Stephanie whispered as the Fosters' big red cat strolled in our direction.

"Me-ow!" Fluffy said again, and actually sniffed the air!

"Is he a cat or a bloodhound?" Patti murmured.

Fluffy was walking faster now, and meowing even louder.

"We'd better get out of here," I said nervously in Kate's ear. "We don't want anyone to find us!" I was hearing my mom's voice, loud and clear, in my own head: "You know the rules," she was saying.

But it was too late. "What's happening, cat?" a boy's voice asked.

"Denny Bright!" Stephanie hissed. We all froze.

And that traitor Fluffy led him straight to us! The cat squeezed into the hedge and started purring and sniffing at my sleeve, where I'd spilled the dip. I guess Fluffy was just another enthusiastic fan of my special recipe! Then the branches parted above our heads, and the Beekmans' light shone onto our faces as Denny Bright peered into the lilac bushes.

Denny saw us right away, of course, and he opened his mouth to speak . . . Kate put her finger to her lips and shook her head. Denny grinned. Then he winked and closed the branches around us!

"Find something in there, son?" Dr. Bright called out.

"Just a cat," Denny answered, walking back to the driveway.

We waited a few seconds, not moving a muscle. Then Kate barely breathed: "Let's get out of here!"

We backed slowly, slowly out of Kate's hedge . . . into the safety of the Fosters' yard. I'd just given a small sigh of relief when two things happened at once. A window creaked open. And an awful barking noise almost scared us to death!

"Morris?" Kate's mom called out on the other side of the hedge. "What *was* that?"

"I think it was the Hunters' dog," Dr. Beekman replied. "Next he'll be knocking over our garbage cans. Bullwinkle, go home!" he thundered.

But it wasn't our dog Bullwinkle at all — he was spending the night in our garage. It was Donald Foster, coughing his head off!

41

Donald coughed and coughed. Then he croaked out his window in a hoarse voice: "*Friends*? More like *Fiends* — from the *Fire* Galaxy! *Hack, hack hack, wheeze. . . .*" I guess Donald had seen the same movie we had. "Were you guys trying to kill me on purpose? *Hack, hack*. Or are you just the lousiest cooks in the world?"

"Sssh!" I hissed.

"Sorry, Donald," Stephanie whispered in his direction. "We'll make it up to you somehow!" Then we streaked for my hedge before Dr. Beekman got it into his head to investigate.

By the time we'd stumbled up my back steps, we were all puffing and panting and giggling!

" 'Next he'll be knocking over garbage cans.' " Kate repeated her father's words. "Can't you just see Donald in our driveway, flinging them around?"

I was opening the door to the kitchen as quietly as I could. "Yeah," I whispered. "In his blue-and-white striped jammies!"

"Did anyone get a good look at him?" Stephanie said in a low voice.

"At Donald in his jammies?" Kate was still giggling.

"No," Stephanie said. "At Denny Bright!"

Now that we were all safely inside, I closed the door and locked it.

"Brown hair, dark eyes — it was too dark out there to see much else," I said.

"I thought it was really nice of him to keep quiet about us," Patti said.

"Nice, for a seventh-grader," Kate said firmly, not ready to throw around any compliments.

"Donald didn't rat on us, either," Stephanie said.

"That's only because he was coughing so hard," I pointed out.

"Bullwinkle! Go Home!" Kate said, imitating her father's stern voice. All four of us cracked up.

The next morning, we went over to Kate's house to meet the Brights — officially, that is. I think that's when Kate started loosening up about Denny.

The Brights were sitting around the Beekmans' dining table eating breakfast when we got there. Dr. Bright stood up right away and shook hands with each of us, beaming the whole time. He's a tall man with a perfectly oval bald head. His head was shaped so exactly like one of Stephanie's make-over punch-outs that I almost burst out laughing — I couldn't help myself. It was so easy to imagine changing his mouth, or his eyebrows . . . Maybe we should design a make-over kit for guys, I thought, with a page of printed mustaches and sideburns — imagine Donald Foster with curly red hair and a mustache!

Mrs. Bright is a small, thin woman with a warm smile and lots of laugh lines around her eyes. Sara is eight — Kate's sister's age. She has round blue eyes and blonde curls, and she *looks* like an angel. But I noticed she was holding her own against Melissa the Monster — no easy job!

Still, it was Denny we all turned to stare at. He was sitting at the end of the table with an empty plate in front of him, and he was smiling, too.

"Denny, this is my daughter, Kate, and her best friends whom we told you about — Lauren Hunter, Stephanie Green, and Patti Jenkins," Mrs. Beekman said.

I held my breath! I halfway expected Denny to say, "As a matter of fact, we met in the hedge." But he came through like a champ.

Denny stood up like his dad, shook hands with us all, and said with a totally straight face, "Hi. I've really been looking forward to meeting you."

Denny's a little taller than Patti and I, and a lot

broader across the shoulders — like a football player. "He probably wrestles with grizzly bears in Moose Jaw," Stephanie said later. He's got dark-brown hair that's a little shaggy and parted on the side; thick, straight eyebrows; and big brown eyes that shade into green sometimes. He's definitely on the cute side of average, and that day he was wearing a plaid flannel shirt and jeans.

"I thought if you girls had time, you could show Denny some of Riverhurst today," Dr. Beekman said. "He can borrow my bike."

"I'm sure he doesn't want to hang — " Kate began.

But Denny interrupted her. "That sounds great to me!" he said.

Kate closed her mouth in surprise. I guess she was expecting him to act like a typical stuck-up seventh-grader who wouldn't want to even cross the street, much less tour the whole town, with a bunch of lowly fifth-graders.

"We'll take him to the mall!" Stephanie said.

"That'd be cool," Denny said. "There aren't too many malls back in Moose Jaw."

"And Charlie's," I said. "The best sodas and ice cream in town," I explained to Denny.

"And maybe Munn's Pond and the Refuge?" Patti suggested shyly. The Riverhurst Wildlife Refuge is loaded with geese and ducks, some raccoons, and even a few deer.

"Excellent idea! So Denny will see that *Canada* isn't the only place that has nature in the raw." Dr. Beekman is funny sometimes.

"Oh, wow! I forgot," Stephanie said. "I promised to have lunch with Nana!" Nana is Stephanie's grandmother, Mrs. Bricker, who was visiting from the city.

"Then why don't we meet at one o'clock?" I said. "On the sidewalk out front. Does that sound okay, Kate?"

"Uh — sure," Kate murmured. She was gazing at Denny as though she couldn't quite make up her mind about him. But the corners of her mouth kept turning up, and I could tell she was beginning to give him the benefit of the doubt.

Chapter
5

By the time Kate rolled her bike out to the sidewalk at one o'clock, she appeared to have decided that Denny Bright was really something special. For Kate, she was positively burbling!

"Denny's pumping up his tires in the garage. You know that box camera I pulled out of your dumpster, Lauren? Denny fixed it! He took the whole thing apart before lunch. He has this set of tiny screwdrivers and wrenches in a leather case that he carries with him *everywhere*. He cleaned the camera and oiled it. He says now it will work perfectly! He knows all about cameras. He's taken thousands of pictures of birds and animals when he's gone camping in Canada. He has a few prints with him, and they're

47

fantastic. He'd like to be a wildlife photographer. Not only that, he's seen *every movie* that exists on videotape!"

I'd never heard Kate be so enthusiastic about anybody, certainly not a seventh-grade boy! But all I said was, "There's probably not too much TV in Moose Jaw."

But Kate didn't even hear me. "In fact, we're going to the foreign-film festival together tomorrow afternoon at the Quad. Denny's already seen one of the movies, the Japanese one made in 1948, but he said it's worth seeing again." Kate finally ran out of breath. Just then Stephanie rode up on her bike from one end of Pine Street, and Patti from the other.

"What are we waiting for?" Stephanie asked.

"Ready!" called Denny Bright. He came coasting down Kate's driveway on Dr. Beekman's ten-speed. He had a camera with a long, telescopic-type lens strapped to his neck, and he was wearing a navy cap that said "Moose Jaw Marauders" across the front. "Lead the way."

Our plan was to start out at the pond, work our way up Main Street, and finish off at the mall where we'd have a slice or two of pizza at the Pizza Palace.

As Patti had said, "We'll kind of ease Denny into town life a step at a time." The Refuge at Munn's Pond is about as close as Riverhurst comes to wide-open wilderness. And the mall is most like the city, with lots of shops and lights and noise and people, especially on Saturdays. Main Street's kind of in between.

So first we biked to the Refuge, which is neat. It looks as though it's been around for a hundred years, at least. The gate at the entrance is made of real tree branches, all twisted together. To get in, you drop a quarter into the little wooden box attached to it. Nobody cheats. Then you push open the gate and walk down a winding dirt path past a real log cabin. On the other side of the cabin are a bunch of wire cages for wild animals that have been hurt. The people who run the Refuge take care of the animals until they've healed. Then they let them go free again.

That day there was a badger in one cage. He stuck just the tip of his nose out of the hole where he was sleeping and pulled it right back in. In another cage there was a raccoon with a bandage on its side. He looked like he was almost healed because he was running all over the place. In the next cage was a hawk with a broken wing in splints, and then two half grown wild turkeys.

"We have lots of these around our house in Moose Jaw," Denny said about the turkeys. He made a weird gobbling sound to get their attention. When they looked up he raised his camera to his eye and snapped a couple of pictures of them. "And plenty of deer, and even a bear once in a while."

"What about elk?" I asked, because I'd seen a program on TV about the elk herds in Canada.

"Yup," Denny nodded. "Those, too. We once found an orphaned baby elk on a camping trip. We brought him home with us and raised him on a baby bottle, until he was old enough to take care of himself. He comes back every summer, to visit."

"Aren't you going to miss all that if you move to Riverhurst?" Patti wondered.

"I guess I'll get used to it here," Denny said. "Besides, it'll be great meeting new people. There are only six kids in my class in Moose Jaw — four boys and two girls."

Patti had brought some stale bread from home, and we fed the geese and ducks on the pond for a while. Denny took more photos of the birds, of us feeding the birds, even of us *without* the birds. Now, Kate wasn't the only one who thought Denny was special. Donald Foster would probably have made jokes about being afraid to photograph us. He would have said something like: "You're so ugly, you'd break the lens," which is his idea of humor. But Denny even lent his camera to Kate for a couple of shots.

Then we rode down to Main Street. First we stopped off at Trendy, which sells rock-star posters and T-shirts. It turned out that Denny likes the rock group Heat as much as we do. He even bought a black T-shirt with the whole group lined up on the front.

We took Denny into Charlie's long enough to show him the antique stained-glass windows and the black marble counter in front of the soda fountain.

He was impressed. "It reminds me of Frank's Cafe in Whitewater," Denny said. "Whitewater's the closest town to Moose Jaw — not more than fifty miles away." I couldn't imagine that. There must be at least *thirty* towns within fifty miles of Riverhurst!

We also looked in at the health club, which has

a pool and tennis courts and a running track. Stephanie's family are members.

After that, we headed out to the mall.

"The mall is great on weekends!" Stephanie told Denny as we pedaled up Roanoke Avenue. "Practically everyone in town is there."

"Yeah, you may not like it," Kate warned him. "It's awfully crowded."

Denny did look a little startled when we stepped through the automatic glass doors into a traffic jam of shoppers, but soon he started to relax and enjoy himself. He loved the Record Emporium, where you can close yourself into a soundproof booth and play tapes as loud as you want. He liked Feathers and Fins, too. Patti's little brother, Horace, is probably their most loyal customer. He's bought most of his creepy-crawlies there: lizards, turtles, slimy spotted salamanders. They're all living in glass tanks in the Jenkinses' den, and Horace studies them, along with caterpillars and moths.

In Romanos Denny picked up more film for his camera and some special film for the old box camera. Then we watched four adorable cocker spaniel puppies tumbling around in the window of Pets of Distinction. And by that time I was starving!

"I'm getting kind of hungry," I said.

"Lauren, isn't there any way to ever fill the Bottomless Pit," Stephanie teased.

I was a little embarrassed, but then Denny agreed with me: "I could use a slice of pizza myself." Didn't I say he's a really nice guy?

So we trooped up the center aisle of the mall to the Pizza Palace.

The Pizza Palace is not exactly a palace. It's one small room with video games on either side of the front door. It has the best pizza in town, though. Lots of kids from Riverhurst Elementary and Middle Schools hang out in there after school and on weekends. We practically always run into somebody we know.

But that day we had the Pizza Palace to ourselves for a change. We ordered a medium double-cheese pizza with pepperoni, meatballs, and olives for the five of us. Meanwhile Denny glued himself to the Alien Attackers game, just like Mark Freedman or Larry Jackson from our class would have done. He dropped in a quarter, and the *bloops* and *bleeps* began. I guess some things are pretty much the same from Riverhurst to Moose Jaw — put a boy and a video game together, and everything else is history.

Kate must have been thinking along the same lines, because she turned to me and whispered, "Video games are like some kind of giant magnets for boys, aren't they?"

Sure enough, about ten seconds later two middle school guys walked in and grabbed Turkey Shoot and Desert Foxes, the games on the other side of the front door. Soon they added plenty of *squawks* and *pows* to Denny's *bloops* and *bleeps*.

Then Stephanie muttered, "Video games may be magnets for boys, but here comes the biggest *boy-magnet* of them all!"

Michelle Olsen was strolling up the center aisle of the mall with Stacy Bennett, and another seventh-grade girl named Kara Turner. Looking over at the Pizza Palace, Michelle spotted the two middle school boys, who happened to be concentrating too hard on their video games to even see her. Aced out by a machine? Michelle frowned and rapped loudly on the window.

As soon as they saw it was Michelle, the boys let go of the joysticks they'd been clutching for dear life and turned their backs on Turkey Shoot and Desert Foxes!

"That's a first!" I said as they rushed out the door.

Patti nodded. "I know. I've never seen a boy disconnect from a video game until he's run out of money."

Kate wrinkled her nose at the circle of seventh-graders around Michelle Olsen. "Denny would never act so goofy!" she said.

"Oh, yeah?" Stephanie murmured.

We swiveled our stools a little to look at Denny. Alien Attackers stood suddenly silent, because Denny Bright was staring practically open-mouthed at Michelle. As the group of kids moved away from him, up the aisle toward the Burger Joint, Denny raised his camera to his eye to follow Michelle through his telescopic lens!

Chapter 6

"Pizza's done!" John the cook announced. He slid the pie out of the oven on his wooden paddle, sliced it up, and set it down on the counter between Kate and me.

I wanted to get started on the pizza. But Kate was watching Denny, so I did, too. And he was still watching Michelle. At last she disappeared around the corner. Then Denny lowered his camera and wandered over to us. He sat down next to Patti, and bit into his slice of pizza.

He managed to be cool for about one solid minute, chewing thoughtfully. Then I guess he couldn't stand it any longer. "Uh . . . did any of you guys happen to notice that girl?" he asked.

"Which one?" Stephanie asked innocently, glancing at Kate out of the corner of her eye.

"The one in the . . . uh . . . pink and green sweater," Denny said.

"Oh, that's Michelle Olsen," Stephanie replied. "She's a seventh-grader at Riverhurst Middle School, cheerleader, beauty queen . . . ," Stephanie began to rattle off Michelle's accomplishments.

But Kate interrupted her. "Michelle's going steady!" she said firmly.

"Oh." Denny picked up his slice of double-cheese pizza and bit into it again.

Somehow I didn't really believe that was the end of it. But what happened next surprised even me.

The Greens have a membership to the health club on Main Street, and on weekends, you can bring guests to swim in the pool. Stephanie had invited Patti, Kate, and me for that Sunday — girls only. Since Kate had gone to the movies with Denny instead, there were only three of us gathered around the diving board that Sunday afternoon.

We jumped off into the deep end and started swimming. Stephanie, Patti, and I had all done a few laps and were fooling around in the shallow end, turning flips, and walking on our hands, when someone tapped my ankle.

I collapsed in the water, then popped up, and wiped my eyes.

"Didn't I see you in the Pizza Palace yesterday?" a voice said. I blinked. Then I almost fainted. It was Michelle Olsen, and she was actually talking to *me*. Stacy Bennett was standing right behind her.

"Yes," Stephanie answered. Now she and Patti were right-side-up, too.

"Do you know who that guy near the door was?" Michelle said. As usual, she looked fantastic. Her bathing suit was a turquoise-blue and black one-piece with a zip front, and her earrings were shells on the top, and starfish on the bottom.

"What guy?" Stephanie asked coolly.

"He had a humongous camera around his neck, and a little navy cap on," Stacy Bennett said. "You couldn't miss him."

Stephanie and I looked at each other. "Oh, *that* guy," she replied. "His name is Denny Bright."

"Does he live in Riverhurst? Or is he visiting somebody? Or what?" Stacy asked.

"What grade is he in?" Michelle demanded before we could answer Stacy.

"He's probably going to move here," I explained. "Right now, he's staying with the Beekmans. Dr. Beekman?" I added, because I was sure Michelle wouldn't know Kate. What seventh-grader would bother to learn any of our names — except Donald and Denny?

"And what grade did you say he's in?" Michelle repeated.

"Seventh," Patti said, getting into the conversation.

"He looks kind of . . . different. He's got a *funny* haircut and that weird cap," Stacy said, " 'Moose Jaw Marauders'?"

Something about the way she said it really got on my nerves. Who cared what Denny dressed like or what kind of haircut he had? He was a great person. But Stephanie was the one who spoke up first.

"He's from Canada," she said sharply. "Moose Jaw is the name of his hometown."

"Because there are mooses around, just like this place is called *River*hurst because of the *river*," I put in.

Michelle and Stacy didn't look impressed.

"All Canadian baseball caps look like that,"

Patti added. "Denny happens to be the . . . *star hitter* for the Moose Jaw Marauders!"

Wo, Patti! Denny an instant baseball star?! Stephanie and I raised our eyebrows at each other — we didn't know Patti had it in her!

"He's also captain of the middle school football team in Moose Jaw," Stephanie said, not to be out-done. "Notice his shoulders? He wrestles, too." I thought that was going a little far. Seventh-grade wrestlers? But then, why not, in Canada?

"Really," said Michelle, flashing her perfect smile. "I wonder . . ."

But we didn't get to find out what she wondered, because she and Stacy were headed for the steps to the dressing rooms.

"What a nerve that girl has!" I said, staring after her.

Stephanie sighed. "I know. Poor Donald, *I* wonder how long strep throat can last."

"Do you think Denny really plays baseball and football?" Patti asked anxiously.

"Do boys play video games?" I answered with a question.

* * *

Every weekday morning, Stephanie, Patti, Kate, and I meet on the corner of Pine Street and Hillcrest so we can ride our bikes to school together. That Monday, Kate was absolutely raving about the foreign film festival — and Denny Bright.

"We had a great time! The Japanese movie was terrific. It's all about this shipwrecked sailor and a mermaid. . . ."

"A mermaid?" I said as we coasted downhill toward Riverhurst Elementary. There are lots of mermaids in books, but I hadn't seen one in any movies, except for little kids' cartoons.

"It was a fantasy," Kate said. "Denny told me that the director had an entire little island off the coast of Japan spray-painted blue to get the right effect. And then the cameraman used a red filter . . ."

Kate can talk for hours about *one scene* in a movie, so I was sort of relieved when Stephanie interrupted. "We ran into Michelle Olsen at the health club yesterday," she said.

"Lucky you!" Kate said, raising her eyes to heaven.

"She was asking questions about Denny," Patti reported.

"She'd ask questions about any boy who didn't drop dead at her feet," Kate said offhandedly. "Which reminds me. Denny has some questions, too. Would you guys mind stopping by my house after school today? The Video Club is having a special meeting, so I won't be around, and Denny wants to know stuff like where to get a haircut, and directions on how to get there. . . ."

"Sure," Patti said. "I'm free this afternoon. I could actually take him around."

"I'd love to postpone another session in the basement," I added.

"I told Dad I'd go grocery shopping with him," Stephanie said. "But not until he gets home from work around six."

So that was how the three of us ended up at Kate's house — without Kate — after school that day.

"I need to buy some new shirts and jeans," Denny told us. We were sitting around the Beekmans' kitchen table, eating brownies and drinking sodas.

"No problem," Stephanie said to Patti and me. "We'll just take him to Snappy Threads, right?" Snappy Threads is a store for boys on Main Street.

"And I want to get a haircut, too," Denny said.

"Cut-Ups, just behind the mall," I told him.

"Great." Denny grinned. Patti, Stephanie, and I looked at each other. This was going to be fun — a real-life make-over!

Our first stop was Cut-Ups. It's this really trendy hair place with pictures of rock groups and movie stars all over the walls. Stephanie pointed to a picture of Chaz, the lead singer from Heat. "How about something like that?" she asked Denny. Chaz has this really great spiky haircut.

"Sure," Denny said.

Larry, the owner, smiled. "I'll do what I can," he told him.

Denny was pretty cute to begin with, but after Larry had finished with him, he looked fabulous! His hair was cut a little like Chaz's — really short on the sides, longer on the top, and moussed so that it looked kind of tousled.

"What do you think?" Denny asked as he studied his reflection in the mirrored wall behind the cash register.

"It looks great!" Patti said.

"You have the perfect hair for it," Stephanie

exclaimed. "Thick and straight." Stephanie had problems with frizzies, herself.

"Definitely cool," I agreed.

Denny looked even cooler after we'd browsed through Snappy Threads. He bought two new pairs of Levi's, a pair of black jeans, and a shirt with flamingos and palm trees on it. He wore the black jeans and the shirt out of the store.

"Charlie's?" Stephanie suggested when we were out on the street. "For a quickie before dinner?"

"Why not?" I said. Those three brownies I'd eaten earlier had made my mouth kind of dry.

It wasn't until all four of us were sitting in our favorite booth, sipping our drinks, that Denny asked *the* question: "So — where do I go to meet kids around here?"

Kids? What were we? Chopped liver? But I knew what he meant — seventh-grade kids. And not just seventh-graders in general: "Like that blonde girl," Denny continued. "What was her name? Michelle? Where does she hang out?"

Stephanie, Patti, and I glanced at each other. What had Kate said? *Answer his questions*.

"Well," I said. "Here at Charlie's sometimes, or at the Pizza Palace. She practices cheerleading after school, too, behind the middle school gym." We'd seen her there just the week before, hopping up and down and waving her pompoms.

"She was asking about you yesterday," Stephanie added.

That certainly got Denny's attention! His eyes opened wide. "What did she want to know?" he practically shouted.

"If you'd be living here. What grade you were in. Where you were from," Stephanie said. She left out the part about the weird cap and the haircut, which had already been taken care of, anyway.

"Really!" Denny beamed, like his dad. "Wow!"

"We told her you were the star hitter on the Moose Jaw baseball team. And captain of the football team. And a wrestler," I added. "Just to give you a boost."

"Uh-oh," Denny said, his grin fading. "I'm afraid we have a problem."

"What problem?" Stephanie began. "Maybe we exaggerated a little, but you. . . ,"

Denny shook his head. "We didn't play baseball in Canada," he said glumly. "And I'm not on a football team, either, because Moose Jaw's too small for one. Even if it weren't too small, the towns around us are too far away to be able to make the games. And I'm too young to wrestle." At least *some* things were the same.

"Bummer," I said. "So what *do* you play?"

"Lacrosse," Denny said. When he noticed our blank expressions, he explained: "You play it with long sticks that have little nets on the ends of them, and a hard rubber ball."

"Lacrosse," I repeated. I thought maybe I'd seen it once on the Sports Channel.

"I've got it!" Stephanie said. "You and Patti are great at baseball, Lauren. You could fill Denny in on it tomorrow afternoon after school. Just to be on the safe side."

"Stephanie! What about our costumes?" I said. "We only have five days to — "

But Denny looked so stricken that I stopped myself. "Tomorrow afternoon would be fine."

From the way Denny smiled I knew I'd done the right thing. But I was a little worried about Kate. Later that evening I called Stephanie to talk to her about it.

"What's Kate going to say?" I asked. "Don't you think she seems sort of . . . well . . . *interested* in Denny herself?"

"A seventh-grader? After all of her speeches?" Stephanie said. "You're getting carried away, Lauren. If Kate thinks of Denny as anything, it's just as a friend."

Like you think of Donald? I thought to myself. But out loud I said, "Yeah, you're probably right."

Chapter
7

As soon as I saw Kate the next morning, though, I knew we were in very deep water.

Kate's never late, but that Tuesday even Stephanie got to the corner before Kate did.

"I don't think this is a good sign." I said uneasily.

"Lau-ren, you worry too much," Stephanie said.

Patti looked at her watch. "Eight-thirty," she said. "If we don't leave soon, we'll be having lunch with Mrs. Wainwright again." Mrs. Wainwright is the principal at Riverhurst Elementary. If you're late more than once, you have to spend lunch hour in her office, which is enough to make even *me* lose my appetite.

"Here she comes," said Stephanie. "Hey, Kate!" she called out. "Step on it!"

Kate stepped on it, all right. She pedaled up Pine to the corner and never slowed down, never even glanced in our direction, even though she had to ride right past us to get to Hillcrest!

"Kate!" Patti and I spluttered.

"Hold on!" Stephanie shouted at her retreating back.

The three of us pedaled like crazy and caught up with her about halfway to school.

"Kate! What's your hurry?" Patti asked with an anxious smile.

"What's the big idea?" Stephanie added crossly.

"As if you didn't know, Stephanie Green!" Kate turned her head just enough to glare at Stephanie. "You didn't want Michelle Olsen to invite Donald to the dance, so you're . . . you're trying to shove *Denny* in her face instead! I heard about the three of you making up that stuff about Denny. And as if that weren't enough, then you had to go and change his hair and redo his wardrobe, too!"

"*Wha-a-at?!!!*" Stephanie, Patti, and I all started babbling at once.

"It was Denny who wanted a new haircut," Patti

pointed out. "And new clothes. We just took him around."

"And Michelle was the one who came over to *us* at the health club, asking all these questions," I stuck in.

"She and Stacy were being so superior that we wanted to make Denny sound as good as we could," Patti said.

"Michelle can't ask Denny to the dance, anyway. He's not a student at Riverhurst Middle School!" I insisted.

"You were the one who told us to help him, Kate!" Stephanie was outraged.

"Hey — wait up, you guys!" I squawked.

Because suddenly Stephanie and Kate were both speeding ahead toward school. One was riding on the sidewalk, the other on the road, and neither of them was looking to the right or to the left.

"I have a feeling we're down to only two characters from a book for the party on Friday," I said glumly to Patti. "What about Tweedledum and Tweedledee?"

And with that we coasted downhill to the bicycle rack.

* * *

70

Stephanie sits in the front row in our class, 5B. Kate and I sit next to each other in the second row, right behind her. Most mornings, we manage to pass at least a couple of notes back and forth between us. But that morning both Kate and Stephanie were model students: no notes and no whispering. They didn't even giggle when Henry Larkin reached into his pants pocket for a pen, and dropped ten or twelve marbles on the floor.

It was awful! The hours seemed to creep by through math and spelling and social studies, while Stephanie in front of me and Kate beside me sat stiff with rage. It made me so nervous that by the time the lunch bell rang at twelve, I wasn't even hungry.

Stephanie's row files out first, then ours, then the third and fourth, and finally Patti's — she sits in the corner in the last row. Usually we hang around the water fountain in the hall until all four of us are out of the room, so we can walk into the cafeteria together. But that day Stephanie absolutely stormed out of class and disappeared down the hall. And Kate didn't even wait for me to stand up before she was gone, too.

When Patti and I got to the cafeteria, Stephanie was standing in line talking to Betsy Chalfin and Barbara Paulsen from 5C. Kate was farther back, sandwiched in between Michael Pastore and Alan Reese from 5A. Neither of them so much as looked at Patti and me.

It was meatball hero day — usually one of my favorites, but I just couldn't work up any enthusiasm. Once Stephanie had gotten served, she followed Betsy and Barbara to their table. Kate went off with Jane Sykes and Sally Mason from our class.

"Now what?" Patti said as we stood with our trays on the edge of the big room.

"We're doomed if we do, and doomed if we don't," I muttered. "Let's just go sit at our regular table," which is just what we did. After a minute or two Mark Freedman, Larry Jackson, and Henry Larkin came to sit with us.

"What's with Kate and Stephanie?" Mark asked.

Patti and I just shrugged. We weren't sure ourselves! "Hey," Larry said. "Have you guys figured out who you're going to be at the party on Friday?" That was another sore topic as far as I was concerned. "I'm going as Long John Silver in *Treasure Island*!" Larry went on. "It'll be dynamite! My mom's lending me a hoop earring and a red scarf, and my little sister has a stuffed parrot that I'm using. I've even worked out a way to give myself a peg-leg!"

Treasure Island was a great idea. Then Mark told us he was going to be some early airplane pilot from *Wings over the World*. Even Henry had come up with a great costume, Huckleberry Finn. "That way I can wear rags and go barefoot," he said, grinning.

I could hear Jenny Carlin all the way on the other side of the cafeteria, holding forth about the length of her custom-designed skirt. And we *still* hadn't come up with anything. The image of Patti and me draped in old sheets was getting clearer and clearer.

When school was finally over that day, Kate was out of there! I was getting kind of mad myself. I knew she had a special meeting of the Video Club, but she could have said something, couldn't she? Even if it was only good-bye!

Stephanie was no better. When Patti and I caught up with her at the bike rack, she said, "I'm not going to be accused of butting into Kate Beekman's business." She glared at Patti and me. "I wash my hands of the whole Denny Bright mess!" Then she rode off in a huff.

I looked at Patti. "That sounds okay to me," I

said. "I wouldn't mind washing my hands of the whole thing either."

She nodded. "Me, too." As far as we were concerned, the Denny Bright make-over had been officially canceled.

Unfortunately, nobody bothered to tell Denny about it.

Later that afternoon, I was down in the basement, as usual, up to my elbows in Hunter family junk, when Bullwinkle started barking his head off. Bullwinkle weighs one hundred thirty pounds. When we got him we thought he was a cocker spaniel, but he turned out to be part Newfoundland. He looks pretty scary, but actually he's about as dangerous as Rocky, my kitten. Still, I thought I'd better get upstairs before he licked somebody to death.

"Lauren?" a voice called from the other side of my front door. I grabbed Bullwinkle by the collar and pulled the door open.

It was Denny. He was wearing his Moose Marauders cap and carrying an old catcher's mitt. "Hi," he said. "I'm here for my baseball lesson."

What could I do? Send him away? After all,

Denny's a person, too. Besides, I'd already told him I'd do it. Life sure was getting complicated.

"Oh-uhh. Hi, Denny," I said. "Okay. Maybe we'd better start out by changing gloves. Playing catcher is kind of hard to learn in one afternoon, and Roger has an old fielder's glove in his room." I trotted into the house for the glove, a bat, and a baseball. Then I led Denny into the backyard and we got down to business.

If you're planning to go into coaching someday, it doesn't hurt to have an older brother. Roger taught me most of what I know before I was six, and I passed it on to Denny.

"All outfielders stand the same way," I told him. "First you've got to face the batter, of course. Your feet should be about as far apart as your shoulders. Bend your knees a little — that's right! Now, rest your hands on them. Keep your head up. When the pitcher throws to the batter, drop your hands from your knees and take a quick step forward. Since we don't have a pitcher, you're going to have to just imagine that part."

When he had the position right, I hit him grounders to the left and grounders to the right. I bunted and hit a bunch of pop flies. Denny started to catch on. He was learning baseball lingo at the same time: stealing bases, double-header, squeeze play, breaking pitch.

And he was *good*. He said catching a ball in a glove was much easier than catching one in a little lacrosse net. I decided to try pitching a few balls to him to see if he could hit. I'm not a bad pitcher, but even so, he managed to slam a few in. I didn't think it would be too hard to convince Michelle Olsen that Denny was a Canadian baseball star. But we were having so much fun we practiced a lot longer than we really had to. It was getting close to dinnertime, and Denny still wasn't showing any signs of losing interest. Suddenly a window creaked open.

"Did you pay this poor guy to help you out with your game, squirt?" It was Donald Foster, peering out of his living room window. He sounded as superior as always and a lot less croaky.

"*I* should be paying *her*," Denny replied firmly. How many boys would admit that?

"Denny Bright, Donald Foster," I said. "Donald, Denny. He may be in your class here next year, Donald."

As Denny gave me back the fielder's glove and walked toward the hedge to talk to Donald, I prayed neither of them would bring up Michelle.

As far as I was concerned that girl had caused more than enough trouble for one week!

Chapter
8

That wasn't the last I heard of baseball practice, though. The next morning Kate waited for me on the corner just long enough to yell, "How *could* you, Lauren?!" Then she tore off in a shower of gravel.

"Excu-u-use me!" I called after her. "Where's Stephanie?" I asked Patti, who was leaning on her bike waiting for me.

"She's halfway to school already," Patti replied, looking pretty miserable.

Brother! So Kate was mad. And Stephanie was mad. Though it seemed to me that Kate was certainly making a major fuss over Denny Bright, for someone who was always telling us *not* to get excited over seventh-graders!

78

We had tests that morning in math and social studies, so we didn't have time to look up from our desks, much less pass any notes. When it was time for lunch, Patti and I didn't even try to track down Kate and Stephanie. Instead, we deliberately sat at Karla Stamos's table, way over in the corner of the cafeteria.

Karla Stamos is the biggest grind at school. She might not be so bad if she'd loosen up once in a while, but she never does. She just talks on and on about how to develop proper study habits, and what a great student she is, and lots of other exciting topics like that. There's no way Patti and I would ever sit with her for fun. But what better message to send Stephanie and Kate? *We'd rather have lunch with Karla Stamos than with you!*

So all through lunch Patti and I listened to Karla go on about how she can write fabulous poetry because she's a very sensitive person. Then she recited two of her own poems to us. One began: "I am a sad, friendless little flower." Meanwhile, Kate had lunch with Jane again, and Stephanie with Betsy. Even if I hadn't been mad at them before, I would have been boiling by the time we'd spent thirty minutes listening to Karla!

When school was out at three, Stephanie headed for the art studio to do silk-screening with Ms. Gilberto, the Riverhurst Elementary School art teacher. Kate was stopped in the hall by Charlie Garner. Charlie's in the Video Club with Kate, and he wanted to talk about a project they'd be working on together. So just Patti and I were at the bike rack when Denny Bright rode down Hillcrest toward Main Street and Charlie's Soda Fountain.

"Hey, Lauren! Patti!" he called out. The Moose Jaw cap was long gone. His haircut was perfection, he was wearing his new shirt and his brand-new black jeans. Michelle Olsen, look out!

"Hey, Denny!" we called back. "Where are you going?"

"Charlie's Soda Fountain!" He waved good-bye and coasted down the street.

"I'll bet Michelle is there!" Patti said. "There's no cheerleading practice this afternoon."

"Want to check it out?" I said eagerly.

Main Street is only a few blocks away from Riverhurst Elementary. By the time we'd pulled our bikes onto the curb opposite Charlie's, Denny had already made his move.

Or Michelle had made hers — it was hard to say which. She was standing on the corner, surrounded by her usual circle of fans: Chuck, Jimmy Coleman, Steve Quinn. The only difference was, this time Denny Bright was in the center of the circle with Michelle.

"Well, I guess he's happy," I said.

"I'm not so sure," Patti murmured. "He looks kind of nervous to me. Like he did when we walked into the mall on Saturday. You know — that 'get me out of here' look."

But then the whole group started strolling toward the steps leading up to Charlie's front door, and we lost sight of Denny behind hulking Chuck Morris.

"Show's over," I said.

Patti nodded. "He's on his own, now," she said.

Patti came home with me that afternoon to help me in the basement. "Four hands are better than two," she said. "Besides, I love looking through old stuff." Good old Patti. If it hadn't been for her I really would have been down in the dumps about the four of us.

We made a platter of peanut butter and jelly

sandwiches, poured two huge glasses full of Cherry Coke, grabbed a bag of potato chips and my tape player, and headed down the stairs.

Between eating and changing tapes, we got quite a lot done. We hauled three gigantic leaf-bags full of old magazines and newspapers to the dumpster, we threw out two rusty toasters, an ancient weed-whacker, a broken coffee grinder, and three old alarm clocks. Then we started in on some of Mom's clothes boxes.

"Look at this red dress with long sleeves!" Patti said, holding it up. "It's satin, isn't it?"

"What about this blue-and-white number with puffed sleeves and a bow?" I giggled. "Totally trendy."

"Is that your phone ringing?" Patti said suddenly.

I turned down the tape player. "Yep, I'll be right back."

I raced up the basement stairs two at a time, but I wasn't fast enough. All I got was a dial tone when I picked the receiver up.

As I clumped back to the basement, Patti called out, "Lauren, I've got an idea for our costumes!"

"What?" I practically jumped down the last five

steps. I'd almost completely given up hope!

"Remember what you said about Tweedledum and Tweedledee?" Patti said. "That made me think about *Alice in Wonderland*! This blue-and-white dress with a bow? It's perfect for Alice. And the red satin dress would be great for the Red Queen!"

"You're absolutely right!" I exclaimed, getting excited. "And somewhere in this mess is a bunny suit, left over from Roger's fourth-grade Easter play, that we could use for the White Rabbit. Only . . . it's too small for either of us." Roger was a pretty tall fourth-grader, but not *that* tall. "And I can't really see Kate or Stephanie in it, can you? In the unlikely event that we're all friends again before Friday?"

Patti shook her head. "I don't know," she said. "It might fit one of them. I was thinking — Horace made a huge model of a tomato hornworm. It's hollow in the middle, so I'm pretty sure we could use it for the Caterpillar. But it wouldn't fit either of us. Although I'm sure it would fit Kate, if she really held her breath. . . ." Kate's the smallest one of us.

"Good try," I said gloomily. "No Kate and no Stephanie. We could still go as Alice and the Red Queen, but we wouldn't make nearly as much of a splash as we would with all four of us."

That's when Bullwinkle went crazy upstairs. "Denny again?" I wondered. I sort of hoped it wasn't. Things were bad enough with Kate. I didn't want to get in even deeper trouble.

But Bullwinkle was frisking around the kitchen this time. Half of our back door is glass-paned, so I could see who was knocking before I opened it: Kate and Stephanie, together again!

"Yes?" I said coolly, peering at them through the glass. "We phoned, but nobody answered," Stephanie said.

"Can we please come in?" Kate asked.

I opened the door. "We're down in the basement," I told them curtly.

Kate and Stephanie followed me down the stairs, to find Patti sitting in the middle of boxes of clothes and gadgets and toys and books. "Hi!" she said when she saw them. "We've come up with a terrific costume idea for the party!" Patti never holds a grudge.

"Let's hear it," said Stephanie.

"Before you tell us, I'd like to say something," Kate announced.

I shrugged my shoulders. "Okay."

"Stephanie came over to my house a little while

ago to talk things out," Kate said. "She made me realize that I wasn't really mad at you guys at all. I was mad at myself for thinking Denny was special. The truth is, he's a typical seventh-grader, and I'm no more ready for seventh-grade boys than Stephanie is!"

"Has he gotten home yet?" I asked her.

"He rode up just as we were leaving," Kate replied.

"Did he say anything about Michelle?" Patti wanted to know.

Kate rolled her eyes. "I think she's asking him to the dance," she said in a low voice.

"How can she? He's not exactly a local!" I said.

"All she has to do is get the principal to make an exception — tell him that Denny will be a student here next year."

"Gross!" I said.

"Who cares?" Kate said, although she obviously *did*.

"What about the party?" Stephanie said quickly to change the subject.

"We'll do *Alice in Wonderland*!" Patti said.

"Excellent!" said Kate. I remembered that it was

her favorite book when we were little.

"You may not be wild about your costumes," Patti warned her.

"Now that the four of us are friends again, I'd be willing to go as the . . . the Caterpillar!" Kate told us. "I'm feeling lower than a worm, anyway."

"It's nice to hear you say that," I said, "because that's exactly who you're going to be!"

"What about me?" Stephanie asked.

"Well," Patti mumbled, "the costume's one of your favorite colors. . . ."

"The Red Queen?" Stephanie queried.

"No-oo-o," I said slowly.

"Not the White Rabbit!" Stephanie shrieked.

"You got it!" I answer.

Chapter
9

On Thursday afternoon, the four of us went to Stephanie's as soon as school was over, so that Mrs. Green could help us alter Mom's dresses to fit Patti as Alice, and me as the Red Queen. Then we rode over to Patti's house, where we managed to squeeze Kate into the tomato caterpillar model. Horace had made it out of chicken wire and an old sheet, so fortunately it gave a little. He hadn't meant it to be worn, of course. But when we promised to buy him a South American box turtle at Feathers and Fins in exchange, he said we could use it, as long as we were careful.

The costume party started at six-thirty on Friday, and would last until nine. None of us had mentioned

Denny to Kate, but when she climbed into Dad's car at six-fifteen, I said, "Is Denny going to the Sadie Hawkins dance?"

"All I know is, he's definitely getting ready for *something*," she said with a sniff. "Straighten out my antennae, okay, Lauren?"

We picked up Stephanie next. She actually looked terrific in Roger's white bunny suit. She'd put on a black vest and was wearing her black leather jacket with red trim on it. "My colors — red, black, and white," she said, waving her long ears at us. "What could be bad?"

And Patti made the ultimate Alice. Her hair was parted in the middle and hanging to her shoulders, and she'd tied a pale blue ribbon around it. She had on the blue-and-white dress, and white shoes and knee socks.

And I'll have to admit I was a pretty great Red Queen, too. I was wearing the red satin dress with long sleeves, a red foil crown Stephanie had made for me, and we'd covered every inch of my skin that showed with one of those colored zinc-oxide sun blocks. In red, of course.

When we stepped through the doors of the elementary school auditorium, it was a little like stepping into a live picture book or a zoo! There were kids dressed as pigs, as cats, and as wolves. There was even somebody dressed as an alligator. There were trolls, and elves, and fairy godmothers, and a Peter Pan. Henry Larkin was there as Huckleberry, and Mark Freedman looked totally sharp in his pilot's uniform.

Then Stephanie poked me. "Get a load of Jenny and Pete!"

Jenny was a ballet dancer, in yards and yards of pink frills. Pete was dressed as an old-fashioned soldier, in a tight red jacket, blue pants, and black boots.

"What are you supposed to be?" Kate asked him.

"Embarrassed!" was his answer. "My mother made me do it!"

Then Patti remembered the fairy tale about the tin soldier who falls in love with a china ballerina. Although Pete didn't look like he was in love — he looked completely bummed out!

Anyway, *we* had a great time. I danced with at least twenty different guys, although I had to be careful not to smear them with sun block. There was tons to eat, and a yummy fruit punch with ice cream in it.

At last, it was time to announce the winners. When Ms. Gilberto stepped up to the microphone, we knew it would be fast, because she gets terrible stage fright.

"Most unusual . . . ," Ms. Gilberto squeaked. "The Troll under the Bridge — Kyle Hubbard." He's a friend of Kate's. They were in the same class last year. We clapped really loudly as he accepted his prize, a book about the planets.

"Most Beautiful Costumes . . . the Dancer and the Steadfast Tin Soldier!" Ms. Gilberto said. "Jenny Carlin and Pete Stone!"

"The most beautiful Pete Stone!" The other guys yelled and whistled and clapped until Pete turned beet red. Jenny and Pete won a book, too, of American painters.

"And Most Imaginative goes to the Alice in Wonderland gang! Stephanie Green, Lauren Hunter, Kate Beekman, and Patti Jenkins!" As Ms. Gilberto handed us our book, an illustrated history of Riverhurst, Kate announced over the microphone: "Sleepover Friends forever!"

After the dance, the sleepover was at Patti's, but Mrs. Jenkins drove us to Kate's first, because Kate had forgotten her glasses. That's when we discovered that Denny Bright was something special after all.

"What's that tent on Donald's lawn?!" Stephanie squealed as we pulled into Kate's driveway.

Two heads poked through the tent flap. "Hey!" Donald and Denny said at once.

"You're well!" Stephanie said to Donald.

"You're not at the dance!" Kate said to Denny.

"No," said Denny. He sounded a little embarrassed. "Donald gave me good advice about, well . . . a certain girl."

"And now . . . Denny's giving me some good advice about camping out," Donald said.

Stephanie rolled up her window and grinned at Kate. "Well?"

"Okay, okay, Denny isn't just your typical seventh-grader," Kate said. Then grinned. "And Donald Foster isn't always, either."

It was great to have the Sleepover Friends on the same wavelength again!

#24 Lauren's New Friend

"Why don't I go back for Bitsy?" I suggested. "Maybe she's having trouble with the faucet or something."

"I'll go with you," said Stephanie, before Mrs. Mason could think of reasons for us not to.

We hurried back up the path, past Blue Jay and the other cabins. There was no sign of Bitsy.

"Maybe she got freaked out about eating with so many people, and she's hiding," Stephanie said.

"She eats in the school cafeteria," I pointed out. Then I remembered Bitsy hunched down under the Beekmans' table.

I bounded up the steps of Cardinal cabin, ready to shove open the door and drag her out from under the bed, or wherever she was, when Stephanie grabbed my arm. "Ssssh!" she barely breathed. "Bitsy's talking to somebody in there! Come on!"

We crept down the steps again to peek into a side window of the cabin. Bitsy was definitely saying *something*, but to whom? She was sitting all alone on her cot. There was nobody else in the room with her.